WITHDRAWN

Copyright © 2021 by Helen Yoon

The sung line *"Good night and joy be to you all"* is from
the traditional song "The Parting Glass."

All rights reserved. No part of this book may be reproduced, transmitted,
or stored in an information retrieval system in any form or by any
means, graphic, electronic, or mechanical, including photocopying, taping,
and recording, without prior written permission from the publisher.

First edition 2021

Library of Congress Catalog Card Number pending
ISBN 978-1-5362-0731-6

21 22 23 24 25 26 LEO 10 9 8 7 6 5 4 3 2 1

Printed in Heshan, Guangdong, China

This book was typeset in American Typewriter.
The illustrations were done in mixed media.

Candlewick Press
99 Dover Street
Somerville, Massachusetts 02144

www.candlewick.com

OFF-LIMITS

Helen Yoon

CANDLEWICK PRESS

and I don't think anyone
would miss one piece of tape.
Just one little teeny-tiny piece.

How about another?
Why, thank you!
Don't mind if I do.

Why, hello, Mr. Lamp!
What a lovely scarf!

Do you know what would look
good with your scarf, Mr. Lamp?

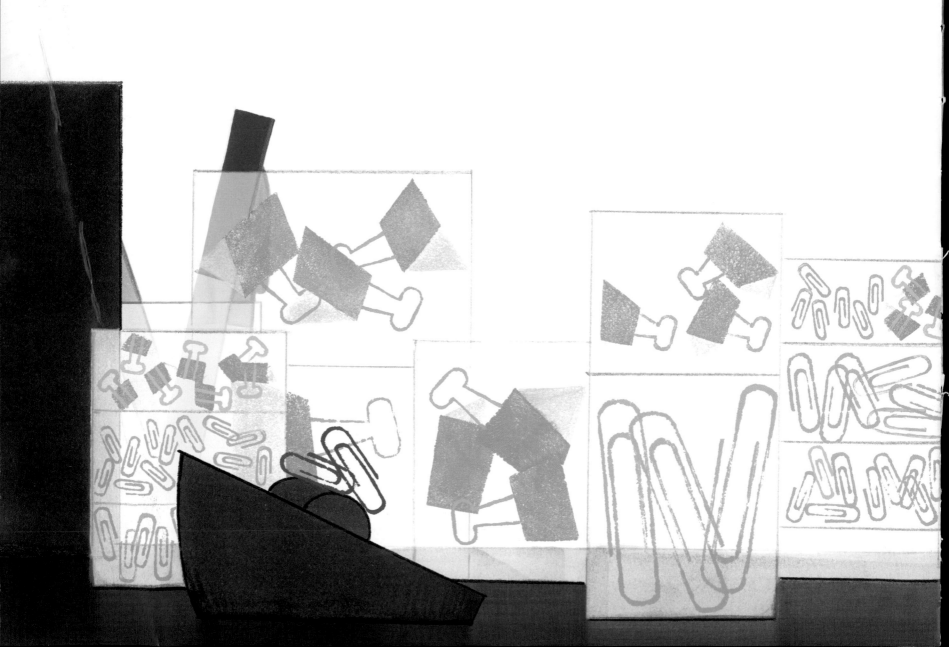

PAPER CLIPS!

PAPER CLIPS AND
BINDER CLIPS!

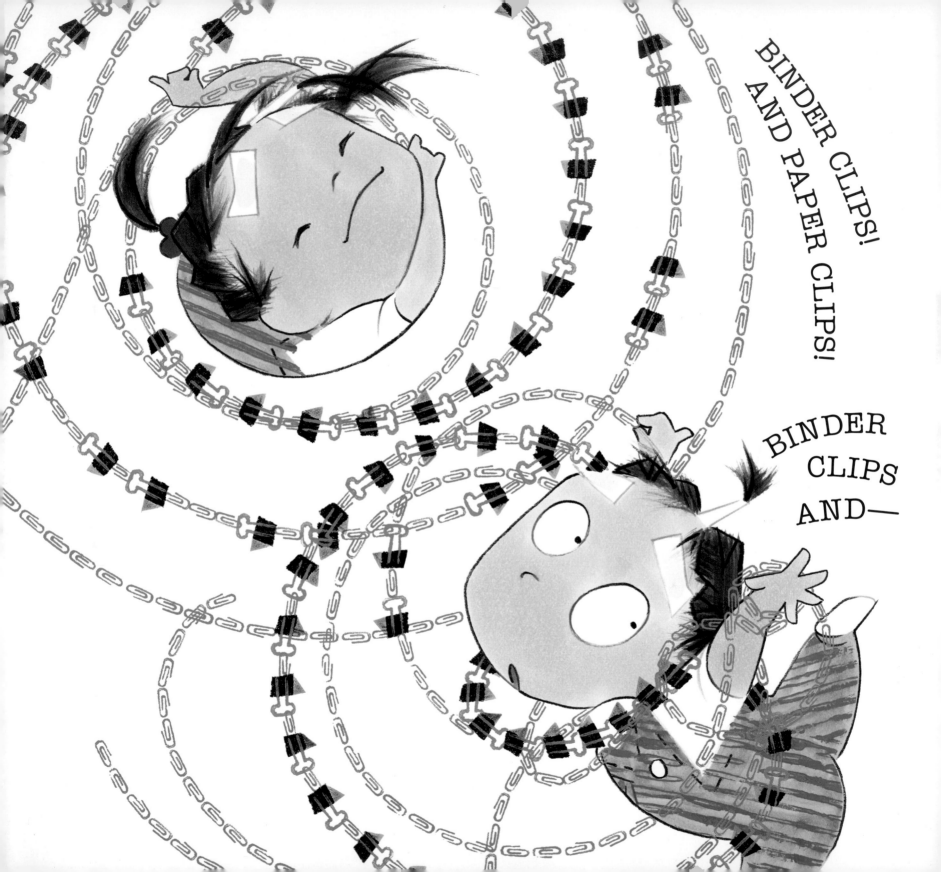

BINDER CLIPS!
AND PAPER CLIPS!

BINDER CLIPS AND—

Pinky. Blue blue.
Yellow yellow yellow.

OFFICE

OFF-LIMITS

I'm in so much trouble . . .